The Carrotastic
Ninja Bunnies

iUniverse books may be ordered through booksellers or by contacting:

iUniverse
1663 Liberty Drive
Bloomington, IN 47403
www.iuniverse.com
844-349-9409

Because of the dynamic nature of the Internet, any web addresses or links contained in this book may have changed since publication and may no longer be valid. The views expressed in this work are solely those of the author and do not necessarily reflect the views of the publisher, and the publisher hereby disclaims any responsibility for them.

ISBN: 978-1-5320-5080-0 (sc)
ISBN: 978-1-5320-5081-7 (e)

Library of Congress Control Number: 2018909670

Print information available on the last page.

iUniverse rev. date: 03/23/2021

The Carrotastic Ninja Bunnies

Ashley Bell

ON A COOL SUNNY DAY, in a tiny, quiet village outside the hustle and bustle of city life, the Villagers were getting ready to harvest their crops. This was to be their biggest harvest yet.

The farmers are awakened by the sun as it starts to rise up. The farmers and their families put their clothes on and eat breakfast before leaving the house. The harvest is important as it was a way of life.

Every harvest, they sell the crops and the livestock they fed until fat to the people in the village. They are given money to help their families and to take care of the farm. The villagers can prepare for winter. Everyone benefits from the harvest.

One farmer and his family go towards their big farm, but when they get there, they noticed something bad. Half of the crops were gone. Their livestock, nearly gone! It happened to the other farms as well. Who could had done this!?

It turns out the Alpha Wolves: the stealthy, sneaky, and agile wolf ninjas had taken most of the harvest overnight. Those Wolves have done this before, but never this bad. Word got out to the villagers. What was anyone to do? Without a good harvest, there wouldn't be enough for anyone.

The Chief of the Village was listening to his people's pleas and decided to send for help. He sent a young boy into the forest for help. The forest was huge and thick with tall trees. He eventually found a huge rabbit hole and shouted loudly for help. Nothing. He shouted again, "HELP!!!!"

A rumble came and out like a rainbow were 4 bunnies: one in Blue, one in Green, one in Orange, and one in Pink. Wearing all black with belts matching their fur, they landed behind the boy. The boy, excitedly began telling the bunnies about the ninja wolves taking their harvest. The bunnies looked at each other on agreement and quickly took the boy back to the village.

They told the boy to be on the lookout for anything strange. They all wait at his house until sunset. The bunnies decide to hideout inside the small barn close by. Night begins to fall, and the villagers are fast asleep. The small, cool autumn breeze brushes against the wheat and rice. They suddenly hear a rustling sound, then a crunching sound. Someone was outside.

The Blue peeked outside and saw some wolf ninjas, in black and red, swiping rows of wheat from the roots. The bunnies jumped out without a sound and quickly attack the wolves. The wolves aren't ready for what would happen next. The Orange stepped forward and blew fire at the wolves. They barely avoid the fire. The Blue stops Orange and uses his water powers and washes them away towards the huge pasture.

Green uses his earth powers and makes the ground move around them. It wakes up the villagers. The ground around them sinks until it becomes a deep hole. The pink uses her powers to send her and the other bunnies out the hole. She blasts the hole with a powerful wind, bouncing around the wolves, hitting them at the walls of the hole.

She then blasts them out into the air, causing them to fall hard towards the ground below. The 4 bunnies surround them. They were going for one more attack, until a black, shadowy figure approaches from the woods by the pasture and quickly, the ninja wolves throw some bombs. As the smoke clears, the wolves disappear along with the shadowy figure. The bunnies hear a voice from the shadows saying, "We shall meet again." They saved the farm and the Blue bunny filled the hole with water, creating a pond as the rest went to the river nearby and took some fish for the pond.

The next morning, the Villagers and The Chief praise the Bunny Ninjas for saving their harvest. Although no one knew where the wolves took the crops and livestock they stole, they were still grateful. In exchange for helping, the boy's family gave the bunnies a basket full of carrots. The Bunnies, who were thankful, bow their heads in respect and left the village, heading home to enjoy a good pot of carrot soup.

CPSIA information can be obtained
at www.ICGtesting.com
Printed in the USA
BVHW020845020721
610881BV00004B/82